Fish and

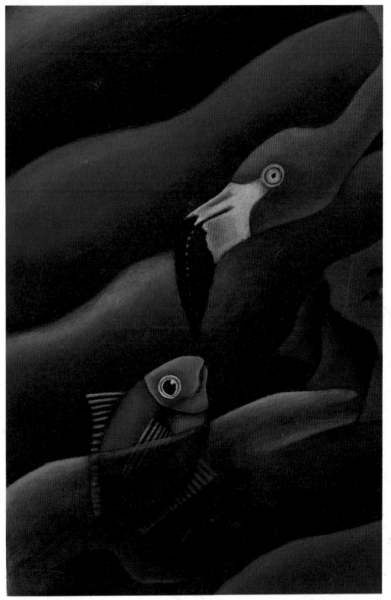

Flamingo

Fish and Flamingo

by **Nancy White Carlstrom** ♦ *Illustrated by* **Lisa Desimini**

Little, Brown and Company   Boston Toronto London

First Edition

Library of Congress Cataloging-in-Publication Data

Carlstrom, Nancy White.
  Fish and Flamingo / by Nancy White Carlstrom ; illustrated by Lisa Desimini.
— 1st ed.
    p. cm.
    Summary: Two unlikely friends, Fish and Flamingo, spend time togetner,
help each other out, and tell stories about their different lives.
    ISBN 0-316-12859-7
{1. Friendship—Fiction. 2. Flamingos—Fiction. 3. Fishes—Fiction.}
I. Desimini, Lisa, ill. II. Title.
PZ7.C21684Fi   1993
{E}—dc20   91-27646

10 9 8 7 6 5 4 3 2 1

NIL

Published simultaneously in Canada
by Little, Brown & Company (Canada) Limited

Printed in Italy

Paintings done in oil on Bristol paper

For Marcia and George Brown —N.W.C.

For my mother and father —L.D.

Once in a place

where the sky slid into the sea

and the sand was hot from morning until night,

a remarkable thing happened.

A fish and a flamingo became friends. How can that be, you ask? Haven't these two been enemies for years? It is true this was not the usual way of such creatures.

But nevertheless, it happened. When the long-legged pink bird stood, head bent, in the water, and the shiny silver-finned fish came, eyes moist, to the surface, they talked. Together. Not of threats or boasts or daring but of ordinary life.

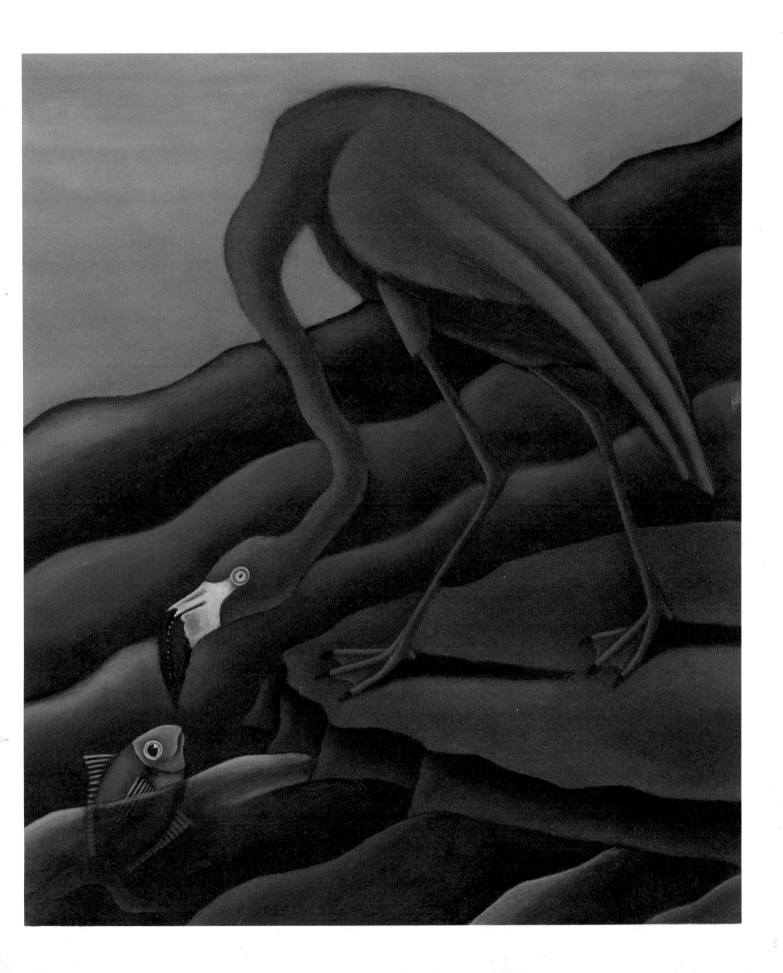

Fish told Flamingo of an underwater world, of swimming on the cool green bottom of the sea, of how it felt to break the surface of

the water at night and float free into the light of a star shining on
the edge of a wave.

Flamingo told Fish about flying when the day was new over the trees of a waking world, and how it felt to catch the breeze and

glide free into the pink of a sunrise growing on the line where
the water meets the sky.

As time passed, this unusual friendship flourished. Once, Flamingo caught her fine, slender foot in the crack of a large rock. Fish pushed in with his firm, slippery body and freed his friend.

Another time, Fish, in great excitement, jumped too far out upon the beach. It was low tide, and surely he would have died if Flamingo had not come to carry him gently back to his watery home. Both Fish and Flamingo agreed that each was a most fortunate creature to enjoy such a friendship.

One day, as Fish swam off, he said, "Flamingo, I wish I could give you a gift. I would like to show you the silver light of a star."

But to himself he asked, "How can one lone fish like myself cause
a star to shine in the day for my friend to see?"

Meanwhile, as Flamingo flew off, she said, "I wish I could give you a gift, Fish. I would like to show you the pink light of a sunrise."

But to herself she asked, "How can one lone flamingo like myself cause the sun to rise over my friend's head for him to see?"

The time came for Flamingo to join hundreds of her own kind
in a journey to a new beach many miles away. Her parting with Fish
was sorrowful.

Flamingo said, "Dear friend, Fish, look to the sky tomorrow
at this time, as I will be flying over your head. I want to
say good-bye."

Fish was sad, but at the same time he was also excited about
seeing his friend fly high in the sky. So he said to the other fish,
"Come here tomorrow and you will see my beautiful friend,
Flamingo, flying in the sky."

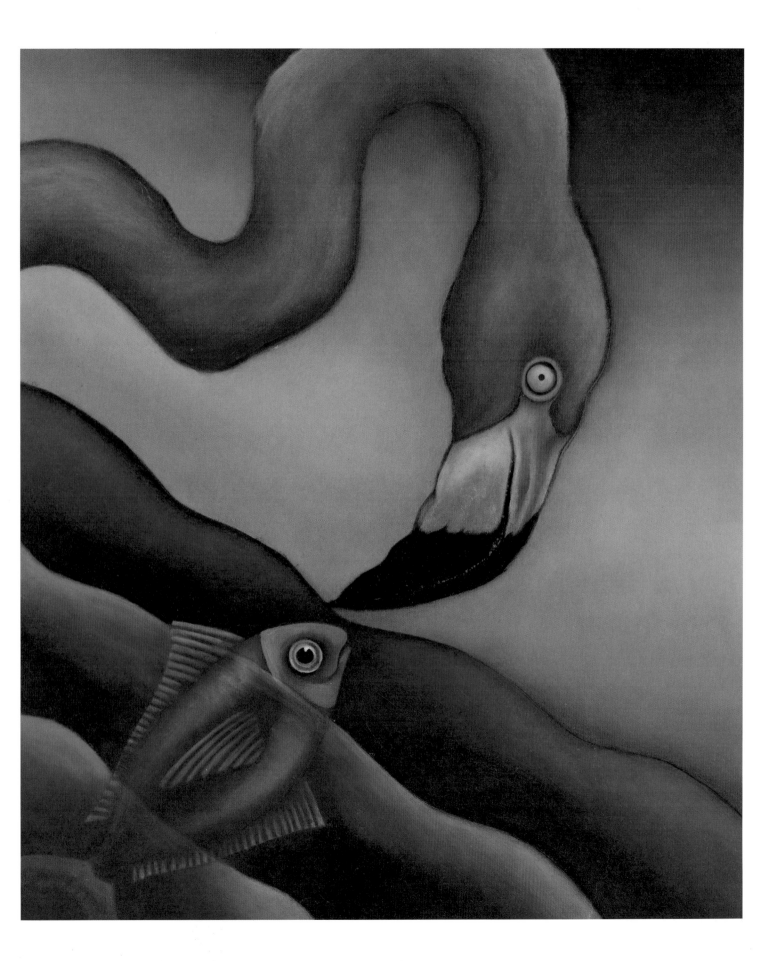

The next morning, Fish and hundreds of his kind gathered near the surface of the water to wait. Suddenly there was a great noise overhead. Fish looked up. He was surprised to see a long line of pink waving through the sky.

"Is that your friend Flamingo?" the other fish asked. "She is much bigger than we thought."

Fish was silent. He did not recognize his friend in the beautiful color

that was spreading as far as the fish could see. And then he remembered.
"That's not my friend Flamingo, but it is her gift. She has given me
a sunrise."

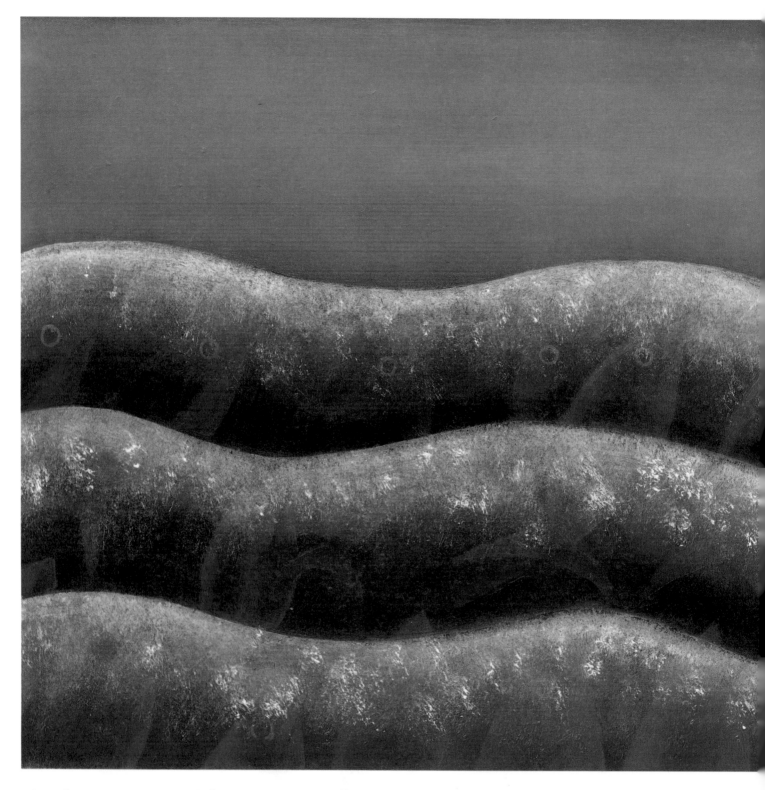

At that moment, Flamingo was flying over. As she looked down to say good-bye to Fish, she was startled to see not one but hundreds of fish in the water below. She strained her eyes to pick out her friend.

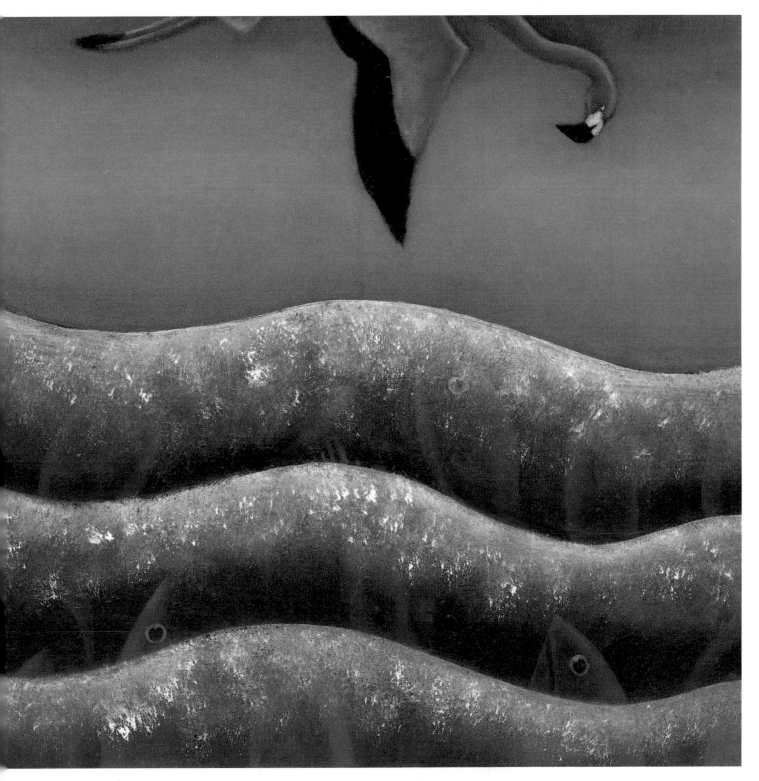

Just then the sun came out from behind a cloud and shone on the waiting fish, turning them into a great silver light.

"Oh, what a friend," said Flamingo. "Fish has given me a star."

Fish never forgot Flamingo and the gift he received from her.
Flamingo never forgot Fish and the gift she received from him.
But neither Fish nor Flamingo knew of the gift each had
given the other.

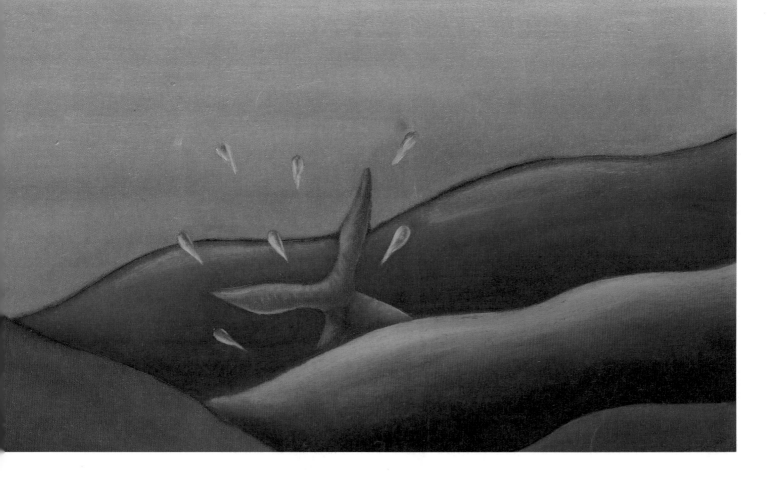

E
C

Carlstrom, Nancy
    White.

Fish and flamingo.

$14.45

DATE			
T-2			

NOBODY KNOWS
I HAVE DELICATE TOES

NOBODY KNOWS
I HAVE DELICATE TOES

by Nancy Patz

Franklin Watts
New York | London
Toronto | Sydney | 1980

Library of Congress Cataloging in Publication Data

Patz, Nancy.
   Nobody knows I have delicate toes.

   SUMMARY: Benjamin and his friend, an elephant,
get in and out of trouble while getting ready for bed.
   [1. Night—Fiction. 2. Elephants—Fiction]
I. Title.
PZ7.P27833No   [E]   79-16304
ISBN 0-531-02392-3
ISBN 0-531-04096-8 lib. bdg.

Also by Nancy Patz
Pumpernickel Tickle and Mean Green Cheese

To Susan and Jeanne

One night just before bedtime
Benjamin and Elephant were busy as usual.

"Get ready for bed now, Benjamin!" Benjamin's mother called.
"Clean up your room and take your bath."

"It's early, Mom!" called Benjamin.

"NOW!" said Benjamin's mother.

"I'd better get ready
for bed, El."

"I'll help you, Benj,"
said Elephant.

"Where does the ball
belong, Benj?"

"Back in the box
in the corner, El."

"I'll bounce the ball
and hop a hop
and *plop!* the ball
goes into the box."

"Good shot, El!"
said Benjamin.

"Where does the orange truck go, Benj?"

"Right up there on the middle shelf."

"I'll help you, Benj," said Elephant.
"I'll jiggle and juggle a bit with my trunk
and tap it and tip it
till *plinkitty-plunk*,
it settles itself away on the shelf."

"I'm a good helper,
aren't I, Benj?"

"You bet, El,"
said Benjamin.

And everything went fine until...

Elephant yelled, "FOUR! THREE! TWO! ONE! BLAST-OFF!"
He zoomed a rocket across the room and...

bumped — THUNK! — into the shelves.
And everything came tumbling down.

Elephant stumbled
     and tripped on his trunk
          and crashed with a thundering roar!

"WHAT'S GOING ON IN THERE,
BENJAMIN?"

"Elephant, you're not helping at all!" fussed
Benjamin. "You're going to get me in trouble."

And Benjamin put the toys away.

"I couldn't have
done it better myself,"
said Elephant.

"HAVE YOU TAKEN
YOUR BATH YET,
BENJAMIN?"

"I think I'd better
take my bath."

"I'll help you, Benj,"
said Elephant.

"I hope this soap is good for my trunk.
I do have a delicate elephant trunk."

"I didn't know that," said Benjamin.

"*Nobody* knows," said Elephant. "And nobody knows
I have delicate toes."

"Nobody knows you have delicate toes?"

"That's right, Benj," said Elephant.

"And nobody sees I have delicate knees!"

"You're kidding me, El!"

"Would I do that?" laughed Elephant.

"Delicate elephant!"

"Elegant nose!"

"Delicate elephant
knees and toes!"

Such a good time
in the tub!
Until . . .

"ARE
YOU
READY
FOR
BED
YET,
BENJAMIN?
I'LL
BE
THERE
IN
A
MINUTE!"

Elephant hid under the water like a submarine.

"I'm practically ready!"
Benjamin hollered.

Then he yelled, "Get moving, El!"

But Elephant was stuck in the tub!

Absolutely stuck in the tub.

Benjamin pushed.

Benjamin tugged.

But he couldn't get Elephant unplugged.

"What are we going to do, Benj?"

"We'll have to think of something, El."

Elephant moaned.

But Benjamin was thinking.

And he got a good idea.

He said, "Pull yourself up
by the bar up there."

"The bar up where?"

"The bar up there."

"I'll try, Benj," said Elephant.

Benjamin gave him a push from the side.

But Elephant stayed stuck.

"BENJAMIN, ARE YOU READY?"

"We've got to think of something, El!"

"I did, but I just forgot it, Benj."

"Elephants never forget, El."

"They do when they're upset, Benj,"
said Elephant.

Elephant was upset.

But Benjamin was thinking.

And he got a good idea.

"I hope this soap
is a slippery soap," said Benjamin.

"I hope so, too," said Elephant.

And together they soaped Elephant all over.

"Let's try it again, El!" Benjamin yelled.

So they pushed and they pulled...

and nothing happened at all.

So they pushed and pulled
some more.

And nothing happened at all.
Until...

SPLUSH!

"I knew we could do it,
El!" laughed Benjamin.

"Me, too, Benj,"
said Elephant.

Elephant slurped the puddles up
and squirted all the water
back into the tub.

They mopped the floor
and got themselves
ready for...

bed.

"Did you take a good bath,
Benjamin?" asked Benjamin's mother.

"You bet, Mom!" said Benjamin.

And Benjamin and Elephant
smiled.